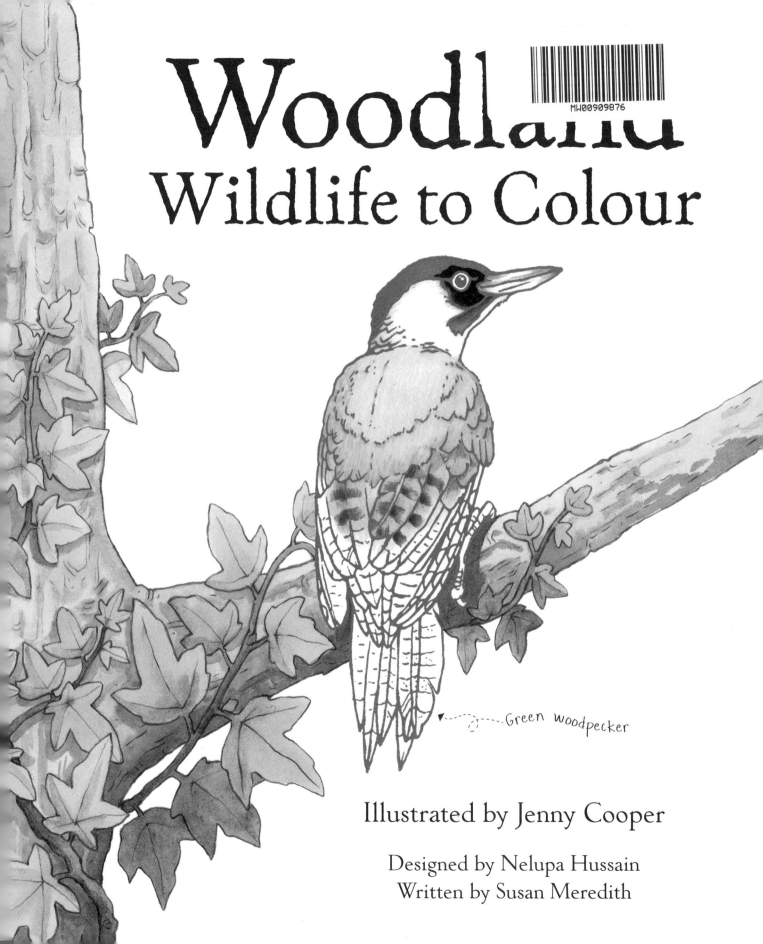

Woodland
Wildlife to Colour

Green woodpecker

Illustrated by Jenny Cooper

Designed by Nelupa Hussain
Written by Susan Meredith

Bluebells and primroses

Bluebells and primroses grow in the woodlands of Europe.

The weight of bluebell flowers makes their stems curve over.

They flower in spring, when they can get the sunlight they need. In summer, the leaves on the trees shut out the sun.

Bluebells have a strong, sweet scent.

In folk tales, the bell-shaped flowers ring out to call fairies to gatherings.

Primroses are among the first flowers to bloom in spring.

Five petals, in two shades of yellow

Eastern chipmunks

Chipmunks belong to the squirrel family. Eastern chipmunks live in woodlands in the east of North America.

They have five black stripes on their back.

Chipmunks pack food into their stretchy cheek pouches. They carry it back to their burrow and hide it there.

Cream stripe above and below eye

Cream stripe between the black ones

Acorn

Entrance to underground burrow

In winter, chipmunks only wake up about once a fortnight to eat from their foodstore.

Holly

There are over 400 different types of holly bush. This type is often called English holly although it grows all over Europe.

Birds shelter in the bushes. Animals can't get at them because of the prickly leaves.

This bird is called a waxwing.

Prickle

The bright red berries are poisonous to people but birds feast on them.

The shiny, dark green leaves stay on the bush all year.

Undersides of leaves are paler green.

Some bushes have leaves with a narrow, pale border.

Blue jays

Blue jays live in central
and eastern North America.

In autumn, they are often seen
near oak trees because they
love to eat acorns.

They have strong beaks
for cracking open nuts
and eating seeds and grains.

Broad tail is edged
with white.

Oak tree

Acorn

Blue jays scream loudly,
often imitating hawks,
to make themselves seem
bigger and frighten off enemies.

Their tail and wing feathers
are sometimes more of a
turquoise blue than their bodies.

Fly agarics

Fly agarics are poisonous mushrooms that grow under birch and spruce trees. They get food from the trees' roots and the trees get water from the mushrooms.

Young fly agarics have rounded caps.

The full-grown mushrooms have broad, flatter caps.

White spots are called 'warts'.

The 'warts' sometimes wash off in the rain.

Birch leaves

People used to poison flies with fly agarics. They mixed them with milk. The flies drank the milk and died.

Painted buntings

Male painted buntings are the most striking birds of southern North America.

They're so bright they look as though they've been painted.

The birds are very shy and try to hide away in bushes.

Male----➤

Males sing a warbling song.

They fight fiercely with other birds who come near their nests.

Females are less vivid than males and harder to spot among leaves.

Female---➤

Young male painted buntings are green, like the females. This helps to keep them safe from enemies.

Large tortoiseshells

Large tortoiseshells are seen in Europe in spring and late summer.

They drink sweet sugary nectar from tree flowers called catkins.

The butterflies' dazzling pattern helps to frighten enemies away.

Blue flashes on the hindwings startle enemies.

Catkin

Large tortoiseshells have four dark spots on this part of their forewings.

Sugar maples

The maple trees of North America and Japan are world-famous for their varied autumn colours.

Each leaf has three main 'veins'.

Vein----▸

Pointed leaves

There are so many maples in Canada that the Canadian flag has a maple leaf on it.

Maple syrup is made from sugar maple trees.

Black and yellow longhorn beetles

Black and yellow longhorn beetles live at the edges of broad paths in European woodlands.

They lay their eggs in old tree stumps and logs.

Longhorns got their name because of their long, horn-like antennae.

They have long legs too.

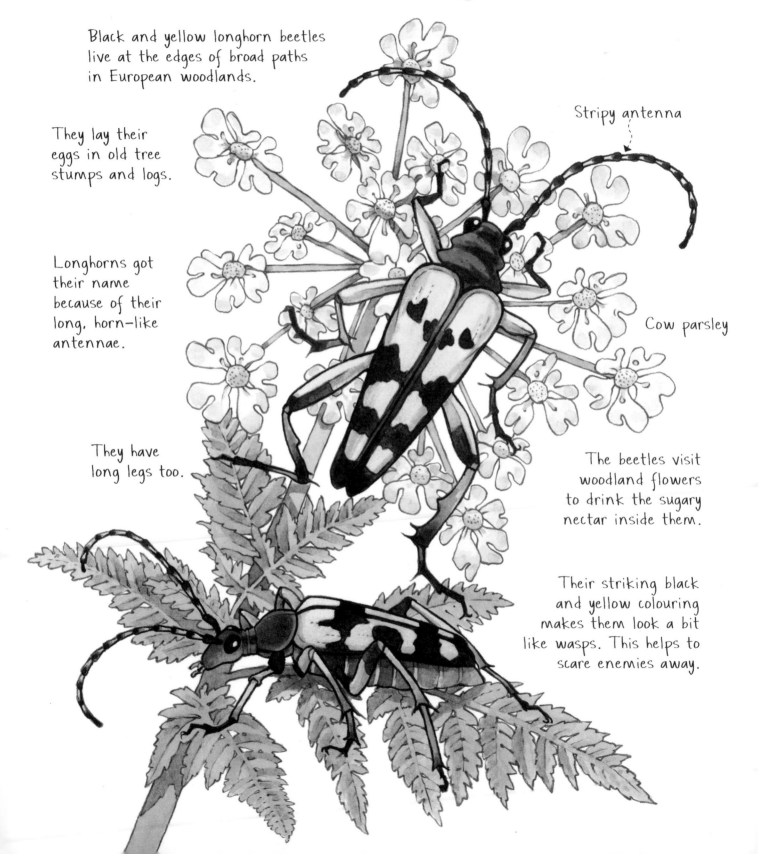

Stripy antenna

Cow parsley

The beetles visit woodland flowers to drink the sugary nectar inside them.

Their striking black and yellow colouring makes them look a bit like wasps. This helps to scare enemies away.

Green woodpeckers

Green woodpeckers live in the woods of Europe and western Asia.

Their green feathers help them to hide in leaves and grass. This keeps them safe from enemies such as hawks.

They drill out nest holes in tree trunks with their sharp, strong beaks.

Nest hole

Males have a red 'moustache'.

Female

Speckled wing feathers

The birds eat ants — about 2,000 a day. They hunt for them on the ground in grassy clearings.

Fallow deer

These shy animals live
mainly in European woodlands.

A male deer
is called a buck.

Only the bucks
have antlers.

Every spring, the antlers
fall off and then regrow,
a little bigger than before.

Stripe along
back and tail

Horseshoe shape
around tail

The deer eat mainly
grass but also
low-hanging leaves.

Their summer coats
are spotted like these.

In winter, the coats
darken and the spots
almost disappear.

A female deer
is called a doe.

Northern leopard frogs

Leopard frogs have spots, like leopards. Northern leopard frogs live in the damp, grassy woodlands of North America.

They are fast movers. They jump into undergrowth or dive into water to escape their enemies.

The stripes along their back are ridges of skin.

Their spots are irregular shapes and have a border round them.

Long toes

Most northern leopard frogs are either green or brown, like these two, but some are both green and brown.

Their colouring helps them to hide in their woodland surroundings.

Purple emperors

These butterflies fly high in the trees of European woods.

They are mainly brown but the males' uppersides shine purple in sunlight.

The males' and females' undersides are almost alike.

←---Female

---Male

The big spots on their wings look like eyes. They frighten enemies away.

←---Male

Purple emperors use their long yellow tongues to drink honeydew – a liquid found on the underside of leaves.

Males also suck up salts and minerals from muddy puddles and animal droppings.

Oak tree

Eyed ladybirds

Eyed ladybirds are beetles that live in pine forests in the north of America, Europe and Asia.

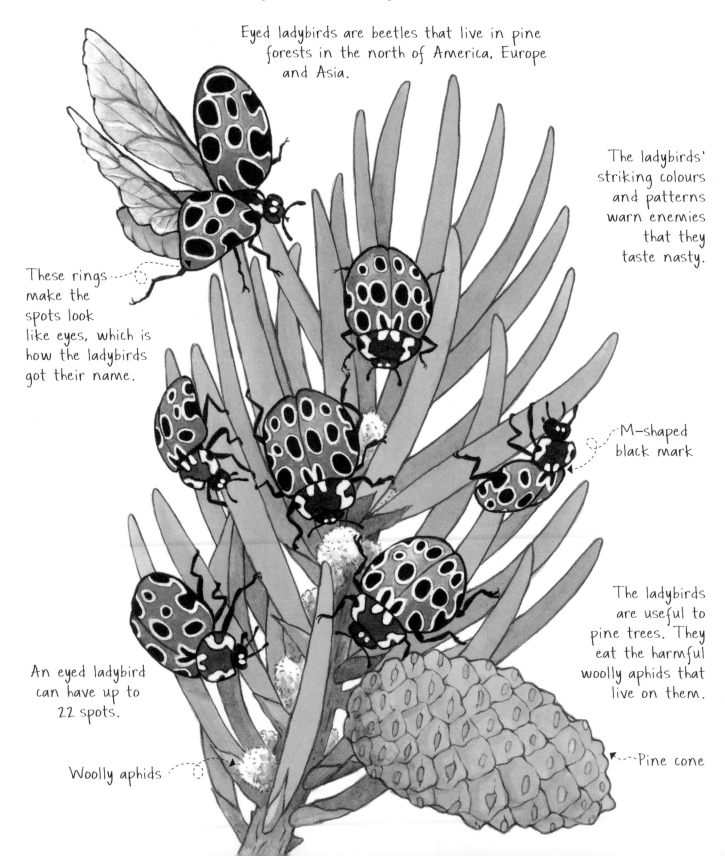

The ladybirds' striking colours and patterns warn enemies that they taste nasty.

These rings make the spots look like eyes, which is how the ladybirds got their name.

M-shaped black mark

The ladybirds are useful to pine trees. They eat the harmful woolly aphids that live on them.

An eyed ladybird can have up to 22 spots.

Woolly aphids

Pine cone

Turkey tails

Turkey tails are mushrooms. They look a bit like turkeys' open tails.

The 'rings' come in all shades of grey and brown, but some also include purple or red.

The mushrooms are found almost all over the world, on dead or diseased trees.

The green areas are algae, which have grown on the mushrooms and the tree.

The trees provide the mushrooms with food.

Turkey tails are a type of 'bracket' or 'shelf' mushroom. They look like shelves growing out of the tree.

Colouring hints and tips

You can use coloured pencils, felt-tip pens, or watercolour paints or pencils to colour in your pictures. If you use watercolours, put some card under your page to stop the rest of the book getting wet.

Coloured pencils

Coloured pencils give a soft effect and are good for doing shading.

To fill in large areas, do lots of lines all going in the same direction.

In areas with shading, press firmly for the dark areas, then gradually reduce the pressure where the colour gets lighter. You can blend different colours together by shading them on top of each other.

Felt-tip pens

For a bolder effect, without much shading, you could use felt-tips.

Use a fine-tipped pen for small or detailed areas.

Watercolours

Make watercolours lighter by adding more water, or darker by adding less.

For distinct colours, let one colour dry before you add the next.

Wet watercolours blur together.

With thanks to Margaret and John Rostron
Digital manipulation by Nick Wakeford

First published in 2012 by Usborne Publishing Ltd, Usborne House, 83-85 Saffron Hill, London EC1N 8RT, England. www.usborne.com